A BLUEBIRD'S FIRST SUMMER

THE STORY OF A YOUNG BLUEBIRD'S
TRUE-TO-LIFE EXPERIENCES

WRITTEN AND ILLUSTRATED BY HELENA CRAVEN

To Ron who attracts **bluebirds** to our farm

Edited by Dorene Scriven and Don Beimborn
Cover Design by Joan Gordon

ISBN 0-9653954-0-5
Copyright © 1996 by Helena Craven

Rt. 1, Box 90
Winnebago, MN 56098

My story began last March when Mom and Dad Bluebird left southern Arkansas to begin their spring migration to the North. They almost starved when a spring snowstorm made it difficult to find food. Just in time, the sun came out and melted the snow and ice. Mom and Dad found some leftover berries and a few insects. They ate, regained their strength, and continued their journey.

Mom and Dad headed north to Minnesota with Mom leading the way. She recognized her home farm. This was the place where she hatched and learned to fly. Last fall, after the bluebirds left to fly south, the farmer cleaned out all the bird houses. He left them open for the winter. Earlier this spring he closed the boxes so they would be ready for use when birds returned to look for nesting places.

     The next few days Mom looked at several bird houses in the
farmer's yard. Mom found some along the fence by the road.
The houses were usually in pairs about twenty-five feet apart.
The farmer knew that tree swallows might nest in one house,
but allow bluebirds to use the other one. The swallows might help
protect the area around both houses from sparrows, wrens, and
other birds that could harm the eggs or the baby bluebirds.

Mom looked at natural holes or cavities in the trees by the creek and in the old grove. She finally chose a bluebird house at the edge of the yard where there was short grass and a hedge nearby. Mom used a mixture of fine and coarse grass to build a nest inside the house. After she finished, Mom and Dad spent a few days catching bugs and relaxing as they guarded their nest.

Mom laid one pale blue egg each morning for five days in a row. After she laid the last egg, Mom began to incubate the eggs to keep them warm. She left the nest only to catch insects, larvae, or worms to eat. Dad watched from perches on tree branches, wires, or from the top of the nest box. One day Dad chased away a house sparrow. The sparrow might break the little eggs so he and his mate could use the birdhouse themselves!

After Mom incubated the eggs for fourteen days, my brothers and I hatched. Because we had no feathers and were so tiny and helpless, Mom sat on us, or brooded us, for several days to keep us warm. Luckily for us, the farmer's wife kept the grass near our house mowed. On the grass, Dad easily found food for us. At the same time, he watched for other birds that might try to harm us.

When we grew enough feathers to keep ourselves warm, both Mom and Dad were kept busy finding food for us. They also carried away our fecal sacs or wastes. Our nests stayed neat and clean. Mom didn't mind when the farmer opened our house to check on us. He knew certain insects, like ants or blowflies, could injure us or make us very sick. Though I was the only female, I still looked like my brothers.

One dark night a raccoon tried to climb the pole that held our house. Fortunately, the farmer put some slippery paint on the pole, so the raccoon couldn't climb up the smooth plastic tube. Snakes, ants, and other crawling predators couldn't get up to our house either. It was good that Mom chose this wooden house instead of a natural cavity in an old tree. If we lived in a tree hole, the raccoon could climb the trunk and reach right into the nest!

Our feathers grew. By the time we were two weeks old, all our flight feathers were nearly full sized. We still had bits of down on our heads. On the eighteenth day after we hatched, my brothers and I heard our parents calling to us from a nearby bush. This was the day we fledged. One by one we flew for the first time. The farmer placed our house so the opening faced the hedge. That way we could fly straight away from the house toward Mom and Dad. We noticed Dad was more brightly colored than Mom.

The day after we fledged, the farmer's wife walked toward a garden to work with her flowers. She didn't know we were in the nearby trees. Dad flew right down in front of her face to warn her to stay away. He did not want her to come near us. The farmer's wife knew what Dad was trying to tell her, so she went to the other side of the yard to work. Mom and Dad went back to feeding us.

After staying nearby for a few days, we moved to other places on the farm. At first Mom and Dad fed us, but then Dad started to teach us to find food ourselves. While Mom started to look for another place to nest, Dad taught us to watch for hawks, cats, and other dangerous animals. Since Dad would soon be helping Mom raise another brood of baby bluebirds, we needed to know how to live safely on our own.

Now it is early fall. Mom and Dad's second brood of baby bluebirds is fully grown. I helped feed the new babies as they grew. Our extended family spent many relaxing days near the farm. Soon we will leave Minnesota to migrate south for the winter. I will come back next spring to nest near the home farm to raise my own family of baby bluebirds!

GLOSSARY

Brood - a group of birds hatched together

Cavities - holes or hollow places

Down - soft fluffy feathers on young birds

Extended family - more than one brood of birds with the same parents

Fecal sac - a white waste pouch of a baby bird

Fledge - to fly for the first time

Flight feathers - adult-size feathers enabling a bird to fly

Incubate - to keep eggs warm by sitting on them until they hatch

Larvae - young, wingless, and often wormlike forms of many insects

Migration - a group of birds moving from one area to a distant area

Predators - animals that hunt other animals for food

Helena Craven is a former teacher
who lives on a southern Minnesota farm
with her husband Ron. She often helps
him as he tends his bluebird houses.

Detailed information on creating a successful bluebird trail is available from the Bluebird Recovery Program (BBRP) of Minnesota, Box 3801, Minneapolis, MN 55403. BBRP is a part of the Minneapolis Chapter of the National Audubon Society. For a tax-deductible donation of $5, this volunteer nonprofit organization will send an initial information packet containing a full-scale plan of the Peterson nest box, a Gilbertson PVC box plan, a predator guard plan, a brochure on trail maintenance, a nesting guide and a predator identification guide. It also contains a quarterly newsletter which is a source of discounted mail-order items such as the adult book *Bluebird Trails - A Guide to Success*.